What love Looks Like

created to be
children's books

Written with love for my dad, mom, husband, children and friends who have shown me what love looks like.

To help you discover your child's love language visit 5lovelanguages.com.

This book was inspired by *The 5 Love Languages*, first published in the United States by Northfield Publishing, 820 N. LaSalle Blvd.,Chicago, IL 60610, copyright © 1992, 1995, 2004, 2010, 2015 by Gary D. Chapman. Used by permission. All rights reserved. The 5 Love Languages is a registered trademark of The Moody Bible Institute of Chicago.

For more info, lesson plans & FREE resources visit:
www.createdtobe.com.au
www.facebook.com/created.to.be.books
www.instagram.com/createdtobebooks

What Love Looks Like
First published in 2015
hardcover published in 2020
Text & illustrations © Nikki Rogers.

US Paperback ISBN 978-1-5009602-7-8
Hardcover ISBN 978-0-6487232-9-5

 **createdtobe.com.au**

For more information about the inspiration behind this book please scan this QR code.

What love Looks Like

Written & illustrated by

NIKKI ROGERS

Did you know that everyone needs to feel loved?
Whether it's a little baby, your mom, and dad,
the leader of a country, a hero, or even a
beautiful princess ...
Everybody needs to know they are loved.

There are lots of things we can do to show others
that we love and appreciate them.
People experience love in many different ways.
Let's have a look together at some of the things
that can make people feel loved!

Words of Affirmation

Some people feel loved and valued the most
when people say kind words to or about them.

"I know my dad loves me because he always says,
'I love you' and calls me 'his princess'.
He reminds me that I'm beautiful and special by
the way he talks to me."

"I love to receive special notes from my friends and to hear my teacher tell me I've done a good job. It makes me feel good inside when people say nice things to me."

Many people really care about the words others say and can be very hurt when unkind words are said about them. That's why we try to use words that encourage and not words that could be hurtful.

Are you a good encourager?

Acts of Service

Some people really appreciate the kind and helpful things that others do for them. It could be cooking, cleaning, helping, fixing, or building. These can be acts of love.

"My mom does lots of things for our family because she loves us. She cooks yummy food and always helps me when I need it. Sometimes I help her hang out the washing because I love her so much."

"My dad helped me build a treehouse and fixed my bike when it didn't work. Sometimes he helps me build great things with blocks.
I know he loves me very much."

People can feel forgotten and unloved if they need help but no one notices or seems to care. Look for ways you can show love by doing something helpful for someone else.

Do you appreciate the kind things people do for you?

Physical Touch

Some people feel especially loved when they are touched in a friendly or loving way.
This may be a pat on the back, a high five or a hug, while others prefer to keep to themselves.

"I feel loved by my dad when he takes me for rides on his back and shoulders. We like to wrestle together and he gives the best bear hugs! I like to be close to him."

"I know my mom loves me because she gives me lots of hugs and kisses. I like to snuggle close to her when we read stories together. I feel safe, cozy, and warm in her arms."

People who like a friendly touch can feel very sad or hurt if someone hits, kicks, or pushes them away. That's why it's important that we only touch people in a friendly way that makes them feel safe and comfortable.

Do you love giving cuddles to your family and friends?

Quality Time

Some people just like to be with the ones they love and feel special when others want to be around them.

"I enjoy going to cafés with my big sister.
I like talking to her about all sorts of things.
I feel loved and special when she spends time with me."

"One of my favourite things is when my uncle plays basketball and other games with me. I like spending time with him. He's lots of fun! "

People who like to have special time with others can feel very sad and unwanted if no one wants to play or talk to them.
We show people that we care by spending time with them and listening when they talk to us.

Do you enjoy doing things with the people you love?

Gifts

Most of us like presents but some people feel especially loved when they receive a gift.

"I know my mom loves me because when we go to the beach we collect shells together. She finds pretty shells and pebbles for me to add to my collection."

"My grandma loves me so much that she sews special gifts for me. It can take her a long time but she likes to make things because she loves me."

It feels good to give someone a gift from the heart. It doesn't have to be big or expensive, just a gift of love. This is why we must be careful with things that belong to others, no matter what they are. To them, they might be valuable treasures that someone has given them.

Do you feel really loved when someone gives you a gift?

Now you know some of the different ways that people show love and feel loved. How do the people in your life show you love?

When we make someone else feel loved it makes us feel good too! What can you do to show your family and friends that you love them?

What makes you feel loved the most?

We were made to love and
be loved beyond measure.
Everyone is unique,
a valuable treasure!

May you always
know you are
loved

To help you discover your child's love language
visit **5lovelanguages.com**

About the Author

Nikki Rogers is a mother, teacher, author and illustrator of children's picture books. Nikki was raised on a farm in Qld, Australia and pursued a career in Primary Education.
In addition to teaching, she has a passion for the arts, writing, drawing and painting. She also enjoys spending time in nature and loves wildlife.
As her desire to have a positive impact on the lives of children merged with her love of art, several beautiful books to inspire and delight children were created.

Nikki currently lives on the Gold Coast with her husband, children and bantam chickens. She has a heart for the less fortunate and desires that her life may glorify God and inspire others to be all they were created to be.

Inspirational Children's Books by Nikki Rogers

 A Beautiful Girl Like You is a lovely book that celebrates the unique beauty found in every girl. With sweet illustrations accompanied by poetry, little girls and big girls will love this book that inspires them to shine the beauty within.

 A Hero Like You was written to inspire children to be everyday heroes by highlighting qualities such as loyalty, compassion, resourcefulness, justice, and courage. What the world needs is a hero like you!

 The Garden In My Heart shares the timeless message that we reap what we sow, and encourages children to plant good things in their heart. We all have a garden that can produce flowers of joy or weeds of bitterness.

 Rainbow Moments is a colorful book that explores some of the ways God can speak to us. It encourages the reader to stop, look, listen and recognize the special moments when God reminds us of His love and promises.

 What Love Looks Like is a delightful story that looks at the many different ways people give and receive love and can help you identify what makes you and others feel loved the most. Inspired by **The 5 Love Languages®**.

 Sooty & Snow is an entertaining cautionary tale about boundaries based on the true story of an adventurous chicken who insists on finding ways to get over the fence. Will Sooty realize the fence is there because she is loved?

 Wilbur the Woolly is a parable about trusting the good shepherd. Follow Wilbur the sheep on his journey as he learns to trust in the shepherd's love for him and discovers that getting his own way isn't always best.

 Born To Stand Out is a color-filled story about Camo the chameleon finding his "true colors". Camo finds that as he steps out in confidence he inspires others to do the same, and the world becomes a more colorful place.

Made in the USA
Middletown, DE
22 February 2023

25376070R00018